The Serpent
of
Shingle
Creek

Swanee Ballman

Top Shelf Books
Jawbone Publishing Corporation
2907 Paddington Way
Kissimmee, Florida 34747
www.JawbonePublishing.com

ISBN 1590940407

THE DISCOVERY

Thomas C. Parker leaned against the fence rail and scanned the 200-acre pasture. Something didn't seem quite right, but he couldn't lay his finger on the problem.

He removed his Stetson and wiped perspiration from his tanned brow. "By gum, the herd is acting strange today. Very strange." He watched a cluster of Cypress cows as they twitched their ears and lowed softly.

He removed his double-barreled shotgun from the scabbard on the side of his saddle. The quarter horse kicked its hoof and bobbed its head up and down.

"Easy, girl," he soothed. "Easy."

He opened the barrel and slid two shells into the chamber. With a final pat on his trusty steed's neck, he walked into the field.

Gathering clouds offered temporary relief from the merciless August sun. Thomas hoped for an afternoon shower to cool his Angus herd, even if it meant another humid evening.

The cows stood at attention as Thomas moved among them. A calf ventured toward him with the curiosity of a toddler. Keeping his eyes focused on the orange grove ahead of him, Thomas reached down and scratched the animal between its ears.

He cursed silently as his boots crushed the dried grass beneath his feet. "Might as well send up flares," he mumbled.

The leaves in one of the tallest and oldest trees rustled over and beyond the wind's force. Something was in the orchard.

With his senses on red alert, he inched forward, still aware of the lowing of the cows behind him. He cocked his head to listen but heard nothing. Not that he expected to hear anything.

He raised his shotgun to shoulder level and proceeded. Perhaps he could finally get the Florida panther that had robbed him of several cows in the past month.

Beads of perspiration dotted his upper lip. His mind pounded a cadence, "Be careful, be careful, be careful."

The leaves on an upper limb seemed fluid as he watched. No panther he had ever hunted caused that kind of motion.

He dared not blink. Whatever shook the limb was causing waves.

A deafening hissing erupted from the treetop. Thomas jumped backwards. His eardrums pounded with pain.

"What in the —" He ran from the grove and fell onto the dried grass, barely missing a foot-high fire ant hill.

This hissing continued, turned to screeching, and grew in intensity. Thomas dropped the shotgun and clapped his hands to his ears.

The ground trembled as the herd raced to the far end of the pasture. For the first time since his brothers left him in the church cemetery alone at midnight, Thomas was frightened.

Time moved in nano-seconds before him. The hissing shrieks seemed to be coming from all directions. Leaves on the upper limbs waltzed to the macabre sound of the creature.

Thomas lowered his Stetson to shield his eyes from the sun's wicked glare. He blinked. He blinked again. This couldn't be happening. Not now. Not to him. Not today.

A green mass streamed from the tree. It flowed along the lower limbs to the trunk and onto the ground. Flowing towards Thomas. Hissing. Flowing.

When the creature had slithered from the tree, Thomas guessed its length to be about twelve feet. Its girth was as thick as 50-year-old cypress tree.

Thomas struggled to a kneeling position. Too shocked to move, he stared at the monstrous serpent that stretched out across the floor of the grove.

Instant and all-encompassing fear choked the cowboy. He couldn't breathe. Paralyzed, he could only watch the massive mountain of snake that moved away from him.

The serpent reared its massive head and stared at Thomas. Its luminous green eyes seemed to focus on the trembling figure in the pasture. The loud hissing grew even louder.

Thomas moaned. His head swirled. Just before he lost consciousness, he looked at the enormous forked tongue that probed the earth from inside arm-length fangs.

"Mister Parker? Mister Parker?"

The voice sounded distant. Was someone looking for him.

"Mister Parker!" The voice grew closer and more familiar.

Thomas opened his eyes and stared at the Palmetto fronds that blocked his view of the figure standing before him.. From this angle he watched the march of an army of fire ants that had reached his shoes and were crawling up the leg of his jeans.

"Mister Parker, you need to get up! Those ants'll eat you alive!"

James Moss, whose father owned the ranch next to the Parker's ranch, hovered over Robert. The teenager extended his hand to help Thomas to his feet.

Thomas staggered as he knocked the ants from his pant leg. He leaned over to retrieve his shotgun.

"No, sir. Don't," James warned. He stepped in front of the rancher and his weapon and retrieved the shotgun. "Are you okay, sir?"

Thomas squinted in the late afternoon sunlight. "I reckon so, James. I reckon so."

James frowned. "I was just herding some strays back from the creek when I saw Shadow trotting down the lane without you. Since he was saddled up, I came to see if you were alright." He reached for Thomas Parker's arm. "Let's get you home."

Thomas slapped his Stetson against his leg to knock the sand from it. "I'm gonna be fine. I don't know why I blacked out. I—" Thomas Parker's eyes grew as large as poker chips. "Jimmy, now I remember! I saw it." He grabbed the teen's arm. "There's a huge serpent in the groves. It just might be what is killing the cows. Not a panther, like your dad and I figured."

James stared at Thomas. "Let me help you back to the house, sir." He pointed over his shoulder. "I tied Shadow to the tree over yonder and –"

Thomas spoke louder. His voice quivered. "Jimmy, I ain't making this up. I saw it. I ain't ever seen anything the likes of it. It was at least twelve feet long and green with glowing eyes." He looked toward the grove. "I walked up to the tree and was ready to shoot a panther from it. The limb started moving. But it wasn't the limb. It was the biggest gall-darned serpent I have ever laid my eyes on." His voice grew shrill. "We gotta find that thing and kill it."

James reached out and grasped his neighbor's arm. "We will," he cooed. "Let's get home now."

Thomas rubbed his chin. "Something caused me to fall. Something —" His eyes sparkled with recognition. "I know! I remember!" The brief smile faded from his lips. "The thing hisses. It's worse than any hurricane I can recollect. So loud it nearly burst my eardrums. The pain was awful. And that's why I fell down. That's why I blacked out." His brows knit into a single line. "You had to hear it. You said you were in the lower pasture."

"No, sir, I sure didn't. Didn't hear a thing." He rubbed the back of his tanned neck. "Come to think of it, I do remember hearing something. I thought it was a wind gust. But it did sound a might strange." A shiver ran along the young man's spine. "I sure don't want to tangle with any 12-foot snake. Let's get out of here."

Thomas nodded. "Let's do just that." He paused to stare one last time into the grove. "But, Jimmy, that … that thing is out there. And we've got to take care of it."

James nodded. "But I think you need lots of help to do that, Mr. Parker. Lots of help."

THE PROOF

Moss-draped red maple trees formed a natural canopy over Shingle Creek. Just where the Creek became a swamp of thick Cypress tress, a small canoe floated aimlessly.

Eric Beauchamp held an oar in one hand and a sandwich in the other. His girlfriend, Ida Mae Long, closed the lid on the picnic basket and nibbled on her sandwich.

She giggled "Don't want to share the rest with the gnats."

"Mighty good lunch, Ida Mae," Eric said as he sank his teeth into a large portion of the bread.

Ida Mae stared at the dark water, blackened by the presence of tannic acid. "I wonder what's underneath the water. I mean, I wonder what's down there looking up at us."

Eric's eyes glistened with mischief. "Oh, I'd say a dozen or so gators are irritated with us."

She snickered. "Ain't so. I ain't heard the first click of a gator yet."

"That's 'cause they've turned off their clickers for the day!" Eric looked serious. "Or maybe – just maybe – that great big ol' serpent that Thomas Parker saw down yonder in his grove has eaten 'em all!"

Ida Mae's blushing cheeks paled. "Don't you go teasing me like that, Eric. That's not funny." She sat up, pulling her shoulder back. "Besides, I believe him. I don't care what you think, Mr. Parker is a respectable rancher and would never make up a story like that."

"Maybe so," said Eric. "But my folks say he hasn't been quite right since Jimmy Moss found him unconscious out in his pasture." Eric sliced the water with the paddle. "Know what I think? I think a snake spooked his horse and when he fell, he hit his head. Then in his mind, the snake was much bigger. After all, nobody else has seen anything like a monster snake." He took another bite from his sandwich. " Don't you think someone else would've seen it by now?"

Concentric ripples floated across the surface of the creek. Ida Mae sat wide-eyed. "Look!" she whispered and pointed. "Look, Eric!" There is something in the water. "Could it be -- ?"

"Oh, yeah?" He picked a morsel of food from his teeth. "Maybe it's the giant fish that swallowed Jonah and it's here to get you!"

Ida Mae clicked her tongue. "Don't you be so mean to me. Maybe there is something scary under the water."

Eric snickered. "Scary? Like a bull frog maybe?" He dismissed her fear with a wave of his hand. "You should come frog giggin' with us some night. Then you'll see so many ripples in the water, you'll think someone is throwing rocks up and down the creek."

"Look!" she sat rigid and focused on the ripples. "There is something there!"

Eric squinted and stared at the surface of the tea-colored water, stained by the decay of vegetation from the trees and swamp. The lazy creek, meandering through the Cypress forest and forming the headwaters of the Florida Everglades, looked innocuous to him.

"Oh, Ida Mae, it's just some turtle waitin' for a bug to comeo near."

Ida Mae shivered. "But what if it's the—"

Eric snickered. "The snake? You really don't think that's a true story, do you?"

She crossed her arms across her chest and frowned. "Uh, huh."

Eric sighed and thrust the oar into the water. "Okay. We'll leave. I need to do some chores this afternoon, anyhow. Before pa gets back from the trading post in Allendale, I need to clean out the barn stalls." He looked at Ida Mae. "Wanna help?"

She nodded in silence as she stared at the water. "I want to go home."

Behind them, the circles grew wider. A herd of turkey vultures gathered on the side of the creek where they feasted on the carcass of an armadillo.

A sudden squawking caught their attention. Ida Mae gasped and turned around. Eric stopped paddling and stared.

Squawking vultures flapped their wings and disappeared into the thickness of the moss. All but one. As the couple watched, a large blob shot from the water, enveloped the vulture, and slipped back in to the bowels of the creek.

Ida Mae slapped her hand over her mouth and screamed between her fingers. Grabbing the sides of the canoe with whitened knuckles, Eric screamed.

"Get me out of here!" Ida Mae begged.

Eric sat rigid and watched the circles approach the canoe.

"Eric!" Ida Mae screamed. "Get us out of here!" She yanked the paddle from his grasp and started paddling toward the clearing where they had left the horse and buggy.

Eric continued to watch the water. "Did you see it? Did you see that head? It was … It was…"

Ida Mae's tears gushed with every blink of her eyes. "I saw it! Help me, Eric!"

He reached behind his seat and picked up the other paddle.

When they reached land, Eric jumped from the canoe and yanked Ida Mae from her perch. As they leaped toward the buggy, the canoe drifted back into the middle of the 30-foot creek.

"The canoe!" Ida Mae shouted.

He cracked the whip and the horse bolted into a trot. "I'll get it later!"

The buggy's wheels clattered over a corduroy bridge made from fallen Cypress trees. The horse raced past a grove filled with dots of pale orange. Back at the creek, a large head again broke the surface of the water. As the massive head raised three feet from the water, luminous green eyes scanning the creek.

In a single lurch, the serpent's head toppled the canoe. The picnic basket disappeared into its jaws just before the dugout flipped upside down.

As quickly as the serpent appeared, it was gone. It melted into the Creek that harbored it. Gone into its watery bunker.

Samuel and Mary Lou Beauchamp finished unloading the cart.

"I sure am glad the trading post got in that new supply of calico," Mary smiled at her husband. "I hope I can make my new dress afore the Bronson weddin'. It's mighty nice not to have to spin cotton right now in this heat."

Samuel nodded. He handed his wife a saddlebag filled with gold coins. "Got a good price for the Herefords. Even the eggs paid well this week." He hoisted a bag of flour over his shoulders. "While the grain was being ground, I walked over to Goold's store and bought some Levi's for both Eric and me."

Mary Lou wiped her sweating palms on her apron. "Jane Makinson told me Goold's is one of the only stores in all of America that even sells them pants."

"Do tell!" Samuel exclaimed. "Well, I s'pose Hamilton Disston and his sugar mill have something to do with that. By the way, I saw the Midland train in town today. Sure spooked the oxen. Good thing I locked the brakes on the cart." He brushed a mosquito from his face. "The engineer was all flustered. Said he had to stop six times this morning to chase cows from the tracks." He winked at his wife. "And you should have seen the lady passengers. All covered with soot, they were. They didn't look too happy."

Mary Lou shook her head. "Riding cart."

Samuel leaned against the porch rail. "Shouldn't Eric be here by now?"

Mary Lou shrugged her shoulders. "How long did it take you to have a picnic with me when you were his age?"

He pushed his Stetson farther back on his head. "Well, I reckon I did eat a might slow. But then, I had lots of things on my mind." He reached forward, grabbed her by the wrists, and pulled her into his embrace. "Still think about the same things."

The buggy tore through the trees. "Pa! Pa!"

"Slow down, boy! You'll lose a wheel like that!" Samuel scolded.

Mary Lou raced from the porch and into the yard.

"What's wrong?" she shouted.

Ida Mae slumped in the seat next to Eric. Her disheveled hair concealed her face but not her whimper.

In three large steps, Samuel reached the horse and grabbed the reins. "Whoa!" he commanded to the exhausted mare.

"We seen it! We seen it!" Eric shouted.

"Seen what?" Samuel reached for Ida Mae just as she dove into his arms.

"The serpent!" Ida Mae screeched. "It almost got us!"

Mary Lou grasped her throat. "No!" she moaned.

Eric fell against the side of the buggy. "Mr. Parker ain't crazy. It's out there, all right."

"What did you see, son? And where?"

Mary Lou wrapped her arms around Ida Mae's shoulders and led her toward the wooden rockers on the porch. Eric clutched his chest and staggered behind them.

Samuel repeated, "What did you see?"

"We were adrift down the creek – out by the Parker pasture. Ida Mae noticed some ripples in the water, but I reckoned it was a turtle. She was scared, so I decided to head back." He crossed his arms over his ribs and leaned forward to catch his breath. He glanced at Ida Mae who rested her head on his mom's shoulder and sobbed quietly. "A bunch of turkey vultures was on the side of the creek. They started flutterin' and squawkin'. We looked back and this ... this ..." He shuddered. "This head came out of the water and swallowed one of them vultures whole. And it hardly even opened it mouth."

A moan formed in Ida Mae's throat and erupted as a discordant scream. "It's gonna eat somebody!"

"Pa. I left the canoe in the creek."

Samuel shook his head. "Don't you worry nary a bit about that."

Eric's eyes wandered from Ida Mae to his mother. "We left the basket out there, too."

Mary Loud brushed her hair form her face. "Baskets can be replaced. People can't. I'll make another one."

Eric glanced over his shoulder toward Shingle Creek. "It's been seen twice now. We gotta kill it."

Samuel smacked a mosquito on his arm. "We will, son. We will."

OSCEOLA'S REVENGE

The soldiers sat in a pickup truck in front of a wooden building. Once a trading post at Shingle Mill, this part of Shingle Creek had always been the low water crossing point.

Glenn Armstrong lifted a bottle of pop to his lips. "It's much better in the winter when it's colder."

His friend picked up his jug. "Why don't you just set the bottles in the creek? That would keep it cooler."

Glenn took a second swig. "Are you kiddin'?" He wiped his lips with the back on his hand. "I ain't gonna chance that the serpent will get to me."

David Greer chuckled. "You jut got back from fighting in the Pacific, almost got your head blown off twice, and you're afraid of some legendary snake? Do you really think that thing could still be alive?" David took a large gulp and burped. "Nobody's seen the thing for what … fifty years? The only time anyone talks about the serpent is around campfires."

Glenn's voice deepened in a sort of threat. "Still, I ain't chancing it." He rested his head against the back window. "Hey, when do you have to report to the base?"

David rubbed his chin. "Day after tomorrow. It's been nice seeing the folks again, but I'm ready to get back to soldiering. Kissimmee is so far from everything. I want some excitement in my life again."

Glenn nodded. "At least there's more to do now than when this was Allendale. "I mean, there's a town now. The rodeo ain't bad. It sure did help the war effort by selling those bonds. I've been thinkin' that I just might join the Silver Spurs when I come home for good." His eyes sparkled. "Beside, those cowgirls do look mighty nice in their outfits!"

David intertwined his fingers behind his neck. "I sure would've loved to have been here when Osceola and his raiding parties came into Kissimmee on Saturday nights. That must've been a sight!"

"Yep. Did you know the town was called Allendale in those days? It wasn't much of a town then. Just a post office, a general store and a tavern. I hear tell that those Injuns got pretty drunk and created a big stir at the bar," said Glenn. "My grandpa used to say that if anything was missing from anybody's house, those Injuns probably took it out to Cypress Island with them on Saturday nights." He burped again. "Wonder if Osceola ever saw the serpent?"

David laughed. "Pshaw! No snake can live that long."

"Well Osceola was known to hide out in remote camps. And always in the wet wilderness areas. Even had runaway slaves that served as interpreters for him, since he didn't do a very good job of speaking English." He sighed. "But then, why should he? The Indians were here first."

"I think he needed to learn the language," said David. "My grandpa said they used to trade with the white man at the frontier posts. Maybe they knew more English than they wanted us pale faces to know."

Glenn lifted his pop bottle and licked the final drops of his drink. "You have to understand that the Indians owned Florida before the Spaniards. They never had diseases like measles, smallpox – even the common cold – before the Spaniards arrived. Then along came the English. Next the French. I can understand why Osceola was a bitter man."

David watched a raccoon as it washed its dinner in the tannic water. "Florida is beautiful. It really has everything. Thick forests. Wide grass prairies. Some spring-fed rivers inland. And warm weather when other parts of the world have bone-chilling cold."

Glenn tapped his fingers on the steering wheel. "Yep! It's like being in the Pacific."

David closed his eyes. "The Pacific without the war."

The men sat on the tailgate of the truck and watched their fishing lines drift in the water. Nothing was biting, although blue gills and crappies should have been at least nibbling.

David took a bite from his sandwich. He threw a small piece into the water near a green-backed heron. The bird picked up the bread and dropped it into the water. He floated next to the morsel. When it drifted away, he picked it up and brought it back to the same spot. He did this several times.

"Would you look at that?" Glenn said. "Why doesn't he just eat the bread?"

David stood and stretched. "He wants something bigger to eat."

"What do you mean?"

"He's using the food as bait. I've seen those green backs do that many times. Just watch."

The glossy green head glistened in the sunlight. His black bill was slightly opened.

A small fish nibbled on the bread. But not for long. The bird shot forward and captured the fish.

"That's amazing!" exclaimed Glenn. "I was bred in Florida, and I ain't never seen that before."

David placed his singer to his lips. "Shhhh," he warned. "We have company."

Like well-trained warriors, the men reached for their 30-06 rifles, chambered a round, and placed their fingers on the safety chambers.

A low scream came from down stream.

Glenn motioned for David to follow him. With

careful and deliberate footing, they crept along the creek bank with their weapons at port arm, The scream grew louder.

"What kind of an animal is that?" David whispered, his eyes never straying from the water. Glenn scanned the treetops. "Don't know."

The screaming stopped.

"Whatever was being attacked is something's dinner." David lowered the rifle to his side. "Might as well go back."

The sounds of the creek ceased. The air weighed heavy in the strange calm.

Glenn grabbed his fishing pole. "Guess I should check the bait." He reached for his bag of minnows. "Hey, did you move the bait bucket?"

David searched the ground near the truck bed. "Nope. Maybe the green back stole them."

"I don't think so. Not unless he brought a whole flock of them." Glenn pointed to the truck. The whole back is loaded with water." He scrunched his nose. "And is stinks here, all of a sudden."

The water rippled.

"You've got a bite!" shouted David.

Glenn slowly reeled in his line. "This is heavy! I must have landed a big one!"

"I'll get the bucket!" David dashed to the cab and yanked open the door.

"Aaaaah!"

David spun around. Shooting from the water was the head of the serpent. It rose like a cobra.

Higher and higher. As it grew taller, green eyes watched the men

"Glenn!" David dove for the shotguns and slid one to David. "Get away!" David warned.

The massive jaws opened. A forked tongue protruded and vibrated. Noise worse than the bombs the men had experienced in Pearl Harbor blared in their directions.

Glenn dropped the rifle and covered his ears with his hands. David grimaced but managed to fire a shot toward the creature.

As the bullet found its target, it jerked and screeched. Its long body arched and opened its mouth wider. Long fangs threatened to strike.

David fired again and hit the serpent in the head just below his right eye. It jerked again, screeched even louder, and dropped into the water.

"I got him! I killed the serpent!" David dropped to his knee and rested the weapon on his leg.

"Glenn stared into the water. "I ain't never seen … It isn't a fairy tale. It did exist."

David sat Indian style on the ground. "Nobody will ever believe us."

Glenn rubbed his ears. "We need to pull it out of the water. I want to see it, anyhow." He found an 8-foot loblolly branch and pulled it from its swampy hiding place. "Shouldn't that thing be floating, or do you reckon it's too heavy?"

David stood and walked toward Glenn. "Be careful. Pleaase, be careful."

"I shot it twice in the head. What could –"

The serpent erupted from the shallow creek. His head propelled above the trees and turned first toward Glenn and then David.

"Retreat!" David shouted as he fumbled for his rifle.

Glenn stumbled backwards toward the truck cab. "Go!" he shouted.

Both men slammed the truck doors and slumped in the seats.

The serpent zoomed from the water. As lightning races across the heavens, the snake appeared in front of the truck. He moved his massive body up the grill and onto the hood.

As he stared into the truck, his giant tongue lunged at the windshield. Hissing and screeching, he opened his mouth wide, completely exposing algae-stained fangs.

Glenn twisted the key in the ignition. Grimacing from the noise, he shifted into drive. The truck jerked and stalled.

"Run it over!" David begged.

Again the engine roared and stalled.

"It's too big!" Glenn moaned. "Can't drive over it. Can't move."

David chambered a round and placed his hand on the window handle.

"No!" Glenn commanded. "It'll get in."

Glenn turned the key once more. He pressed hard on the horn.

The serpent bolted backwards and raced across the clearing.

"Shoot it now!"

David yanked open the door and aimed the rifle. He fired once. Twice.

"Glenn leapt from the driver's seat. "Did you get it?"

David's ears ached. A shiver ran down his spine and shook his entire body. "Can't say. But I'm not gonna go in there to find out."

"Glenn slipped back into the truck. "We're gonna get help."

David slid into his set. "I think I'm ready to report for duty. This is a strange enemy. One I don't want to know."

TOURISTS AND TERRORS

The mini-van stopped at the traffic light at Main and Monument in downtown Kissimmee.

"I want to go to Disney again," whined a child strapped into a safety seat.

"I want to plat mini-golf," the ten-year old brother announced.

"Let's do something we can't do in New York. Let's go for an airboat ride," Mr. Stan Barriman suggested.

Doris Barriman studied a small tourist map of Kissimmee. "Turn left and go over the railroad tracks. Then we can see Lake Tohopa ... Tohopakaliga."

Stan steered the van past an old movie theater and hotel. "Wonder why nobody restores those old buildings. I'll bet there's a wealth of history behind those doors."

Doris read from a brochure. "Tohopakeliga means 'Sleeping Tiger.' Must be an Indian name." She patted the brochure. "And look! The airboat ride goes into a swamp at Shingle Creek. That creek got its name because early settlers cut the cypress trees and made shingles out of them."

Ten-year-old Jonathan sat forward. "Cool! We're going into a swamp? I'll bet there's alligators all over the place!"

Doris looked at her husband and smiled. "Gators and turtles and snakes. Oh,my!"

Stan joined her chorus. "Gators, and turtles, and snakes. Oh, my!"

The toddler clapped his hands. "Gators and tuttles, and shnakes. Oh, my!"

They drove along the west bank of the lake. Fishing boats dotted the lake. "I read somewhere that this lake is the second largest inland lake in the state. People come from all over the world to fish here," Doris said.

"Look!" shouted Jonathan. "There's an airboat!" He pressed his nose to the window. "That's cool. Let's go there now!"

Stan turned his head and winked at his son. "That's the plan, my man!"

Stan sat in the elevated seat just in front of the propeller. Doris held Tony and David wriggled in the seat next to her.

"Have a good ride!" said the airboat ride employee as he pushed the boat away from the dock.

As they moved slowly along the creek, Jonathan dropped his hand into the tea-colored water. Doris tapped his leg. "Get your hand inside this boat. Didn't you hear the man back there?

You want to keep that hand, don't you?"

Jonathan pouted. "I don't see anything. There are supposed to be a bunch of alligators."

As Stan pushed the throttle forward, the boat moved faster. "I think we'll see some. Just be patient!" he yelled over the roar of the motor.

As they moved into Shingle Creek, Stan slowed the boat. He looked into the trees and saw terns and herons. A pair of Sandhill Cranes and their offspring stood at attention at the water's edge and clicked a warning to leave them alone.

"Over there!" Doris pointed to the creek bank. Wet sand flew from a hole. "What is doing that?"

The creature backed from his dig and turned its head inside its armored body.

"Is that an armadillo?" asked Jonathan, his voice high with excitement. "I need a picture of that!" He reached into his pocket and pulled out his disposable camera. "That's so cool!"

Down stream a school of minnows flickered through the dark water, Behind them swam a white catfish, its mouth opened for its catch.

"Hey, Dad!" Jonathan shouted. "Look at those eyes over there! Is that an alligator?"

Stan turned the boat in the direction his son pointed. "Could be. It's eye is big enough."

"Now, boys," Doris warned, "you really don't need to get any closer than this. Remember the guy back at the pier warned you not to disturb an alligator nests."

Stan saluted his wife. "Yes ma'am. We'll just sit here and watch for a minute. Okay?"

Doris hugged little David and nodded her approval.

The head submerged beneath the dark water, leaving mere ripples to confirm its presence.

Aw! Do you think it'll come up again, Dad?"

Stan shrugged his shoulders. "I don't have a clue. Let's go on toward the swamp and see what's in there."

Streams of light struggled to pierce through the Spanish moss that choked the trees. Doris shivered. "This place gives me the creeps."

Stan laughed. "Where's your sense of adventure, woman?"

She brushed a swarm of gnats from her face. "In the mall. I get all of the adventure I need shopping."

Jonathan leaned over the side of the boat and peered into the water. "I sure wish I could see what's down there." He looked over to the grove of Cypress trees. "Do you think alligators live in there? How do they move through those ugly roots?"

Stan lifted his baseball cap and wiped beads of sweat from his brow. "I'm sure they're good at getting around here. They know all of the hiding places. And I'll bet we've passed any number of them, and they all see us."

A mosquito bit Doris on the wrist. She slapped

it and blood stained her arm. "Okay, I've now had the jungle experience and I'm ready to return to civilization." She glanced at her watch. "We have ten minutes to return this boat before we're charged for another hour."

"I guess we should turn around." Stan patted Jonathan's shoulder. "Now, hasn't this been fun?"

Jonathan nodded, his attention focused on the ripples in the water. "Dad," he pointed to the side of the boat, "there are those ripples again. Do you think there's another gator around here?"

"Hmm, maybe so." He looked at Doris, whose frown crimpled her forehead. "Can we just stay a minute or so to see what's there?"

"Two minutes. No longer."

The motor purred softly as the boat floated in the middle of the small stream.

Jonathan drummed his fingers on the side of the boat. "Where is it?"

Doris slid closer to the center. "Those things can't jump into a boat, can they?"

The ripples moved closer to the boat. Birds in overhanging limbs flapped their wings and disappeared.

"Stan." Doris stared into the creek. "Don't you think —"

The boat rocked as the serpent shot from the water. He hovered five feet above the creak. Turning his head from side to side, he studied the intruders.

Doris and Jonathan screamed in unison. David whimpered and buried his face in his mom's chest.

Stan shifted the throttle into reverse and backed into a Cypress tree. He maneuvered the boat so that it was headed away from the creature.

The serpent, still staring at them, moved with ease toward the boat. He opened his mouth. Green fangs opened to expose his long forked tongue. He threw his head back and screeched. When he hisses, he spit on Jonathan.

"Dad!" the boy cried.

"Hold him, Doris!" Stan screamed. "I'm heading out!"

He pushed the throttle forward as far as it would go. The airboat jolted, then threw out a spray of water as it sped from the creek.

A small fishing boar blocked their exit from the creek into Lake Tohopakeliga. "Move! Get out of the way!" Stan yelled, his arms flailing in all directions. "There's a monster in there.

"Slow down, man!" ordered the one fisher-man. "You're gonna get yourself killed!"

The airboat bounced past them. "It's coming this way. Leave!" Stan pleaded as they passed.

The fisherman noted the wide-eyes of the man and the hysteria of his family. "Do you suppose they saw the serpent?" he asked his fishing partner.

The partner reeled in his line. "I think it's wise for us to accept what they just said. Just in case."

The fisherman nodded. He looked up through the canopy of cypress, "Storm's brewing, anyhow."

The serpent hasn't been spotted for months. Some evenings out at Shingle Creek, a strange hissing can be heard. Beyond the sound of happily screaming tourists as they frolic in the buffet of vacation thrills, local residents hear something strange out by Shingle Creek. Some say it is just the purr of engines as airplanes fly over the creek from Kissimmee airport. Others explain the noise as the sound of traffic humming along busy Route 192 that carries cars from the Gulf of Mexico to the Atlantic Ocean.

But at night, the old-time residents still stay in their homes and close the drapes. They know. It could be the announcement of an uninvited guest.

Other books by Swanee Ballman:

Tamarind
The Monster of Boggy Creek
The Stranger I Call Grandma: A Story
    about Alzheimer's Disease
Mary and Martha's Dinner Guest
The Very First Lord's Supper
The Chocolate Kingdom Caper
Cockadoodlemoo

All titles may be viewed at
www.JawbonePublishing.com